A MAGIC CIRCLE BOOK

THE TROUBLES OF KINGS:
TWO TALES FROM AFRICA

retold by **LETTA SCHATZ**

illustrated by **JOHN FREAS**

THEODORE CLYMER
SENIOR AUTHOR, READING 360

GINN AND COMPANY
A XEROX COMPANY

TORTOISE
CROWNS
THE
ELEPHANT

Long, long ago, there was great trouble in a faraway land. A huge Elephant was loose in the countryside, and wherever he went, trouble went with him. He trampled people's farms. He gobbled up crops.. He toppled down houses. He muddied the water holes and then drank them dry.

Never had anyone seen an Elephant so huge and troublesome as this one. Even the oldest, oldest, oldest men agreed that he was the worst Elephant they had ever known.

4

Many brave hunters went out to find the great Elephant, but his bellow was so fearfully thunderous that even they trembled when they heard him. Many turned and ran away. Only the very bravest stayed and tried to kill the Elephant, but even they did not succeed. Their spear stabs seemed like mosquito stings to the huge beast.

Then the King sent out troops of his very best soldiers, but they did no better than the hunters.

So the Elephant continued to go his wild way, plundering, thundering, trampling, toppling, smashing, and gobbling. Soon there were very few farms that the Elephant had not visited. The people were hungry and thirsty. Their King grew more and more worried. Something must be done to save the people.

The King thought and thought. He called in the wisest of the wise old men to help him decide what to do. At last he made an announcement. To anyone who could stop the Elephant from spoiling the countryside, the King would give his daughter in marriage.

This extraordinary news spread from farm to farm, from village to village, and from town to town. Everywhere people gathered and chattered and wondered about it.

The King would give his daughter in marriage! Imagine that! It would take a brave man, a very brave man, to stop the great plundering, thundering Elephant. Who was brave enough to stop the Elephant? Could such a man be found?

Many men boasted of their bravery. And for every man who boasted, there were four more who swore that they were even braver. The more they boasted, the braver they felt. Many hunters prepared to hunt the great Elephant. Each swore that he would be the one to marry the King's daughter.

The blacksmiths of the country had never been so busy. Day and night their fires blazed bright as they forged spears for the hunters. Never had spears like these been seen. Some hunters wanted their spears extra long. Others wanted their spears extra sharp. Still others wanted their spears extra strong. Never had longer, stronger, sharper spears been made.

The magicians, too, were busy. Hunter after hunter came to them, begging for magic charms to help in the hunt. The magicians prepared the most powerful charms they could.

From village to village all over the land, drums could be heard drumming. The hunters danced their hunter's dance and sang their hunter's song, and all the people cheered them on as they got ready for the hunt.

At last the hunters set out to find the great Elephant. Some had spears ten feet long, others had spears twenty, thirty, or forty feet long. Some had spears sharper than the sharpest thorn, sharper than a bee's sting, sharper than a snake's fangs. Some had spears thicker than a man's leg.

But the longest, strongest, sharpest spears did not help. The most magical charms did not help. The Elephant turned on his attackers and bellowed his fearful, thunderous bellow, and even the bravest of the brave did not stay to attack again. Some hunters were trampled by the angry Elephant. Some were trampled by other hunters. Some turned back without even seeing the Elephant when they heard just how fearful he was.

At last there was not a hunter left who was willing to try. It seemed that nobody could be found to stop the great troublesome Elephant from spoiling the land.

Now it happened that Tortoise had heard of the King's promise, and when Tortoise saw the King's daughter, he decided that he must be the one to marry her. Never had he seen a more beautiful girl.

Tortoise went to the palace and bowed flat before the King.

"Oh, Royal Highness! May the crown stay long on your head," said Tortoise. "I have come to help you. I can save you from the great troublesome Elephant."

Everyone began to laugh. This was a big boast from one so small. Tortoise save them? Even the smallest spear was bigger than he!

"But first I must be sure," Tortoise said. "If I stop the Elephant from spoiling your kingdom, will you give your daughter to be my wife?"

"I have given my promise," said the King. "A King's promise needs no repeating. He who stops the Elephant shall marry my daughter."

10

"Thank you, Your Royal Highness," said Tortoise.
"There are a few things I will need, of course. . . ."

"I have hundreds of spears of every size, hundreds of swords and hunting knives. Choose what you wish," said the King.

"Oh, no! I do not need spears or swords or knives. That is not what I have in mind," said Tortoise. "I want some of your richest robes. And the great golden chain you wear. And your crown. And . . ."

As Tortoise went on, the people began to murmur. Everyone knew that Tortoise was a tricky fellow. What was he up to? What trick did he have in mind now? Tortoise's voice grew lower and lower as he spoke to the King. The people could no longer hear what he said. Tortoise whispered his plan and the King listened, sometimes nodding, sometimes frowning. Once the King even smiled.

When Tortoise finished talking, the King began to give orders: Do this! Bring that! Call this person! Send for that person! Get this! Pack that! At once!

12

After three days of flurry and bustle, Tortoise set out. He rode the King's best horse, and behind him was a long, long line of servants, each carrying a great load on his head. There were drummers. There were buglers. There were fanners.

The people watched them go by and wondered still more. What could tricky Tortoise be up to?

But the King gave them no chance to stand and wonder. Again the commands began: Do this! Bring that! Send for twenty men! Forty men! Eighty men! Quickly, quickly! Hurry, hurry!

Tortoise and his great train of followers traveled and traveled. Wherever they went, they asked for word of the huge troublesome Elephant. Had he been seen here? When? Which way had he gone? At last they were told exactly where he could be found.

Tortoise sat very straight on the King's horse. In his hand he carried the King's golden staff. Tortoise commanded the buglers to play. He commanded the drummers to drum. Then, with bugles playing and drums drumming, the procession marched through the forest toward the huge Elephant.

14

Closer and closer they came. Closer and closer to the great wild Elephant. Now they could see him. Truly he was tremendous. Never had they seen so huge a beast!

The buglers trembled so, they could hardly blow.
The drumsticks rattled in the drummers' hands. The
fanners shook so hard that their fans waved up a wind.
The servants wanted to turn and run. But Tortoise did
not seem frightened. He calmly marched on towards
the huge Elephant.

"Play!" Tortoise commanded. "Play as you have
never played before!"

The huge Elephant lifted his great gray head. He
stared at the strange procession coming toward him
through the forest. Could these be hunters? Could
they? There was neither a spear nor a sword to be
seen. Besides, hunters come quietly, not with bugles
and drums.

The Elephant listened. The buglers blew such
lovely tunes. The drummers drummed such lively
rhythms. The music pleased his great Elephant ears.
He stood still and listened.

16

Closer and closer came the procession. Then it stopped. A servant helped Tortoise from his horse and alone he went toward the Elephant. Tortoise bowed flat before the great beast.

"Hail, oh Royal Highness!" Tortoise cried. "Long live the King! May the crown stay long upon your head!"

The huge Elephant looked very puzzled.

"Oh, great Elephant," Tortoise continued, "most mighty of beasts! We have come to ask you to be our King. Our own King has died. None but you can take his place. In all the land, there is no one greater or mightier than you."

The great Elephant looked pleased. He lifted his great gray head proudly.

"Here, oh Royal Highness. We have brought your golden staff. We have brought your crown. We have brought the great golden chain. We have brought necklaces of coral. We have brought robes of the finest cloth." Tortoise signaled to the servants, and the gifts were brought to the huge Elephant and spread out for him to see.

18

"Oh, most mighty Elephant, we beg of you," Tortoise pleaded. "Will you return with us and be our King?"

The Elephant looked at the rich gifts spread out before him. He looked at the long line of royal servants. He looked at the buglers and drummers making music just for him. He looked at Tortoise bowing before him.

The Elephant bent his head slowly, a proud kingly nod. Of course, the vain beast thought. It was right that they ask him to be their King. Quite right. What Tortoise said was plainly true. There was no one greater, mightier, more kingly than he.

With buglers blowing, drummers drumming, and twenty fanners fanning the great Elephant, they started back. They traveled and traveled. At last they neared the great royal city. Tortoise sent some of the servants ahead.

"We must tell the people that their King is coming," Tortoise told the Elephant. "They will wish to prepare to greet you."

Soon the servants returned. "Everything has been done," they told Tortoise. "Everything has been done as you said it must be. The people are ready to greet the great Elephant."

20

How proudly the huge Elephant walked as they entered the royal city. His head was held royally high, and on it perched the King's golden crown. He wore great flowing robes of the finest cloth. Round his huge neck hung the great golden chain and countless necklaces of coral. In his trunk he proudly grasped the King's royal staff and waved it high for all to see.

Twenty fanners fanned him as he walked. Ten umbrella carriers carried a huge royal umbrella to shade him from the sun. The royal buglers blew. The royal drummers drummed. The Elephant proudly marched through the town.

The roadway was lined with people. When they saw the Elephant, they began to cheer.

"The King comes! Hail! oh Royal Highness! Hail mightiest of mighty! Hail kingliest of Kings!"

The Elephant held his head even higher. Proudly he waved the royal staff and strutted toward the palace with the drummers and buglers leading the way.

In front of the palace, a platform had been built. It was covered with velvet cloths and leopard skins.

"We have built this for you, oh Royal Highness," Tortoise told the Elephant, "so that all your people may see you and bow low to greet you. We hope it pleases you, oh King!"

The Elephant gave a proud royal nod.

"Will your Royal Highness please stand upon it so that all may see you?" Tortoise begged.

Looking prouder than ever, with his head and trunk held royally high, the Elephant climbed onto his extra special royal platform.

There was a loud crack! And a loud crash! And
the huge Elephant disappeared from sight!

As Tortoise had ordered, the platform had been built of very thin wood and it covered a very deep pit. Tortoise smiled to himself. The King's men had done well. The great Elephant bellowed and struggled, but he could not get out of the pit. The Elephant was caught in Tortoise's trap.

How the people cheered! They were saved! Saved from the huge troublesome Elephant! The King appeared at a palace window. With him was his beautiful daughter. At the sight of the King, the cheering grew even louder. The people had pretended to cheer the Elephant. That had been part of Tortoise's plan. But now they really cheered.

When the people stopped cheering, they began to murmur again. What of the King's daughter? Must she now marry Tortoise? Must so beautiful a girl marry so small and ugly a creature? Surely the King would not agree.

25

The King asked that Tortoise be brought before him. The people waited to hear what their King would say.

"You have done well, Tortoise," said the King. "By your cleverness you have trapped the troublesome Elephant. You have done what the bravest hunters could not do. I have given my promise. Here is my daughter. She shall be your wife."

As the King had promised, so it came to be.

THE
KING'S
SILENT
SON

In long ago times there was a King who had only one son. The boy was handsome and good, as fine a son as any king could wish for. Yet the King was sad, for his son was silent. The boy had never spoken a word. Not one sound had he ever uttered. The King had tried and tried to find some way to help his son. The royal physicians had tried, and the wisest old elders had tried, and the whole royal household had tried. Still the King's son was silent.

One day the King called all the people to the great square by the palace. "I will give half my kingdom," said he, "half my riches, half my robes, half my farms, half my towns — half of everything I own — to anyone who can make my son speak."

28

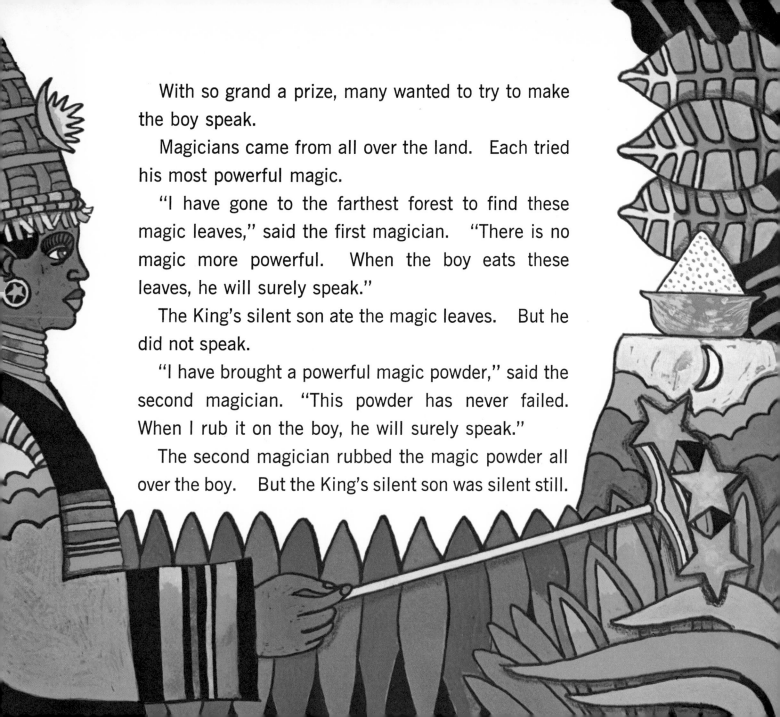

With so grand a prize, many wanted to try to make the boy speak.

Magicians came from all over the land. Each tried his most powerful magic.

"I have gone to the farthest forest to find these magic leaves," said the first magician. "There is no magic more powerful. When the boy eats these leaves, he will surely speak."

The King's silent son ate the magic leaves. But he did not speak.

"I have brought a powerful magic powder," said the second magician. "This powder has never failed. When I rub it on the boy, he will surely speak."

The second magician rubbed the magic powder all over the boy. But the King's silent son was silent still.

Magician after magician came and tried. At last the most magical magician in all the land arrived. He mixed his most magical brews. He chanted his most magical chants. For three days and three nights he worked his magic. But the King's silent son was as silent as ever. The magicians had failed.

Then the best drummers in all the land came to the King's palace.

"We can make your son speak," the drummers said to the King.

The drummers began to drum on their drums. Never had anyone heard such drumming. The people of the town stopped what they were doing and came running to the palace. Everyone who heard the drums wanted to dance. The King danced. His wives danced. His soldiers danced. His servants danced. Even his son danced. The King's silent son danced and danced.

30

Then the drummers began to sing such a catchy song that everyone who heard it just had to sing. The King sang. His wives sang. His soldiers sang. His servants sang. But the boy did not sing. The King's silent son was silent still. The drummers had failed.

Then the best elephant hunters in all the land came to the King's palace.

"We can make your son speak," said the hunters to the King.

The elephant hunters took the silent son to their hunting camp deep in the woods. Early the next morning they set out on their hunt. Soon they found some huge elephant tracks. The hunters smiled.

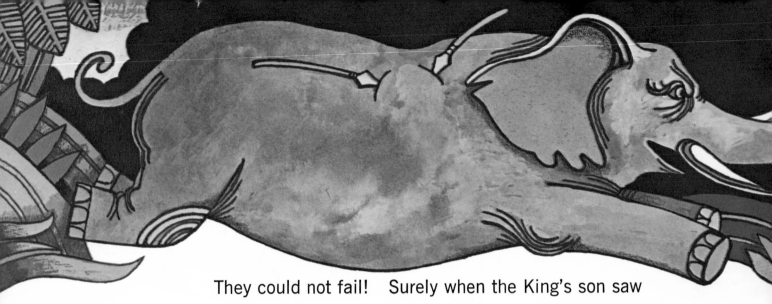

They could not fail!   Surely when the King's son saw
a huge elephant charging toward him, he would cry
out in fright.   Then half the kingdom would be theirs.

They crept toward the elephant.   The first hunter
threw his spear.   The elephant was wounded and
bellowed in anger.   It turned and charged right toward
the hunters, right toward the hunters and the King's
silent son.   Then all the other hunters threw their
spears at the elephant, shouting and yelling as loud
as they could.   They waited for the King's silent son
to cry out.

32

The wounded elephant thundered closer. Its angry bellows filled the forest. Its sharp tusks almost touched the King's son as it charged past. But the boy remained as silent as ever. The elephant hunters had failed.

After watching all this from above, Thunder, himself, came down from the sky.

"I can make your son speak," Thunder said to the King. "The hunters did not frighten him. But I will make him cry out in fright."

The King smiled. All the people nodded their heads. Surely if anybody could make the boy speak, mighty Thunder would be the one.

Thunder took the King's son to his home in the sky. Thunder thundered so loud that all the world shook.

Louder

and LOUDER

AND LOUDER

For seven days and nights he thundered. He called on Lightning to help with great flashes of fire. The King's son shook and shivered and trembled. But still he remained as silent as ever. Even mighty Thunder had failed.

Then Rooster came before the King. "I can make your son speak," Rooster said.

The King stared at Rooster. In those days Rooster did not have his beautiful feathers or bright red comb. He was a very plain, common-looking bird.

All the people began to laugh. Surely this was a joke. How could this little bird make the boy speak when even mighty Thunder had failed?

"You?" exclaimed the King. "You say that you can make my son speak? Magicians, drummers, elephant hunters, even mighty Thunder himself — all have tried and failed. Do you think that you can do what they could not?"

Rooster nodded his head. "I can make your son speak," he said again. "If you will let the boy come with me for just one day, and bid him to do whatever I tell him to do, he shall speak."

The King sighed. "All have tried and failed. What have I to lose? Tomorrow you may have your chance."

Early the next morning Rooster came for the boy. Rooster carried no magic charms, no wonderful drums, or long sharp spears. All he brought was a very old basket and a broken calabash bowl. The basket was so old it had no bottom, and the calabash bowl was broken in half.

The people laughed softly to themselves when they saw Rooster. Did he plan to cure the boy with only a bottomless basket and a broken bowl?

"Come," Rooster commanded the boy. "I wish to catch some fish for my dinner. You must serve me and be my helper. Carry this basket and follow me."

36

Rooster led the way down to the river. The King's silent son followed silently. He was a good boy, used to obedience, and he had been told that he must do as Rooster said.

Rooster walked along the riverbank until he found a muddy hole where the mudfish lived. "Stop!" Rooster said. "This is the place. Here we will surely catch plenty of fish. Now mind! You must hold the basket tightly — with both hands!"

Rooster waded into the river. He bent over and dipped his calabash bowl into the water, trying to catch a fish. Again and again the bowl came out empty. Again and again Rooster tried. The King's silent son watched patiently. And then, at last, the calabash came up with a fat mudfish wriggling inside. "Ah! A fine fat fish!" Rooster exclaimed, and he held the fish up proudly. "A fine fat fish for my dinner!"

"Quickly," he commanded the boy, "come here with the basket! And remember — hold it tightly! That basket must not tip or slip or drop. You must not take a hand off. Not even for a moment!"

Rooster flipped the fish into the basket. But since the basket had no bottom, the fish fell right back into the river. Before it could swim away, Rooster caught it again in his calabash bowl.

"Aha! My luck is changing!" Rooster exclaimed. "Another fine fat fish! Two fine fat fish for my dinner!"

The King's silent son was sadly puzzled. His master for the day was making a terrible mistake. And there was no way that the boy could tell him. He could not even point. Had not Rooster commanded that both hands must hold the basket and never let go? The King's silent son tried to make a sign that something was wrong. He twitched his shoulders. He wrinkled his face. But Rooster did not seem to notice. He just went on catching the same fish over and over, and each time he exclaimed, "Aha! Another fine fat fish for my dinner!"

All morning this went on. The sun rose higher and higher. The day grew hotter and hotter. And still Rooster continued to catch the same fish and toss it into the bottomless basket. And still the King's son held the basket with two hands and watched in silent misery. He no longer tried to make signs to Rooster for he could see that it was useless.

At last, after Rooster had caught the same fish one hundred and one times, he straightened up and said, "This should be enough. Let me look into the basket. By now it must surely be filled with fish. What a feast of fine fat fish I shall feed my family tonight!"

Holding the fish as if ready to drop it in, Rooster looked into the basket.

"Ah wu!" he cried out. "Where are my fish? All my fine fat fish?"

Rooster grabbed the basket from the boy and peered inside, as if looking for some place where the fish might be hiding.

"What have you done with them?" Rooster demanded. "Where have they gone? Where are all my fine fat fish?"

The King's silent son pointed at the basket. The unhappy boy tried to show by signs that it had no bottom, that it could not hold even one fish, much less one hundred and one. But Rooster only grew angrier.

"Thief!" Rooster shouted. "Who would think it? The King's son a thief! For shame! What will your father say when I tell him? Stealing fish from a poor hungry rooster! You who have food enough to feed five thousand!"

In misery the King's son pointed and motioned, but Rooster grabbed him by the ear, crying, "Fish stealer! All the town must hear of this!"

Rooster started back toward the town, dragging the unhappy boy along and insulting him loudly as they went.

"Thief! Thief! One hundred times thief! Oh, the shame you bring on your father!"

They passed some farmers, who looked up curiously.

"Fish stealer!" Rooster shouted again.

This was more than the King's son could bear. He began to cry. The King's silent **son** began to cry!

Rooster seemed to notice nothing. "Thief! Fish stealer!" he repeated.

"It is not true,"
the unhappy boy burst out.
"I did not steal!
I am no thief!

How dare you call me,
the King's son,
a thief?

How dare you,
how DARE you,
HOW **DARE** YOU
INSULT ME?"

Rooster still strutted on as if nothing unusual had happened, and dragged the unhappy boy behind him. The farmers followed in open-mouthed wonder.

As they neared the town, they met more and more people along the way. Each time someone new came into sight, Rooster again began to shout insults at the boy.

"Thief! Stealer of fish! Spoiler of your father's name!"

Each time the boy grew angrier. Each time he answered more loudly than before.

"It is not true!
I did not steal!
I am no thief!

How dare you call me, the King's son, a thief?
How dare you, how dare you,
HOW DARE YOU INSULT ME?

NO ONE could do the task you asked!
You cannot keep fish in a bottomless basket!"

Soon they had a whole train of people following them, gaping in wonder. The King's silent son was speaking! The King's silent son was SHOUTING!

Through the town gates and into the town they went, the Rooster shouting insults, the King's son shouting back, the people following them.

"Thief! Thief! One hundred times thief!"

"It is not true!
I did not steal."

"Thief! Thief!"

"How dare you call me,
the King's son, a thief?
How dare you, how DARE you,
HOW DARE YOU INSULT ME?"

"Shame on you! Stealer of fish!"

"**NO ONE** could do the task you asked!
You cannot keep fish
in a bottomless basket!"

The people crowded through the palace gates. The King heard the hubbub and came to see what was happening. The King could not believe it. His silent son was speaking. No. Not speaking. Shouting! Words poured from the boy's mouth as if a locked storehouse had burst open.

"It is not true!
I did not steal!
I am no thief!
How dare you call me,
the King's son, a thief?
How dare you, how DARE you,
how **DARE** you insult me?
The magicians came.
They did not insult me!
The drummers came.
They did not insult me!
I went with the hunters.
They did not insult me!
I went with Thunder.
He did not insult me!
No one could do the task you asked!
You cannot keep fish
in a bottomless basket."

The King listened in amazement.   Surely this was
a miracle! Was this Rooster's doing?   Had little
Rooster succeeded where the mighty had failed?

Rooster bowed before the King. And when the King heard how Rooster had tricked the boy and worked this miracle with only a bottomless basket and a broken calabash bowl, he was more amazed than ever.

The King called for a great celebration so that all could share his happiness on this happiest of days. And the King did not forget his promise. He gave Rooster half his riches, half his robes, half his farms, half his towns, half of everything he owned.

Thus, when you see a rooster strutting proudly about with many colored feathers and a bright red comb on his head, you will know how this came to be. The beautiful feathers are the rich robes that the King gave him and the bright red comb is the crown. These were Rooster's reward for making the King's silent son speak at last.

48